Voices from the Dead

VOICES FROM THE DEAD

By Lozano Gilabert

Published by Timbercrest Publishing

Edited by Erik D'Souza
Cover design by Carlos Lozano-Gilabert
Copy-edited by Lyn Ayre

Copyright © 2020 Carlos Lozano-Gilabert

ISBN: 978-1-9992824-5-5

First Edition

License Notes

To Cecy, Cami & Carlitos,

for being who they are.

To Carmela, Marisa & Pablo

for making me who I am.

Table of Contents

Veteran

During supper, the topic came up again. The four of them were around the table: Mom, Dad, little Bettie, and James. This time the usual clatter of silverware against porcelain stopped.

"What did you just say?" Mom asked.

"C'est la guerre, mieux vaut prevenir que guérir," Jimmy repeated.

"I didn't know they were teaching you French at school," Mom said, and caught Dad's eyes, knowing full well Jimmy didn't have that subject in grade six.

Jimmy didn't answer anything and, after a little while, raised some beef stew to his mouth.

"Are there any other words or phrases that you've learned?" Asked Mom.

"Bien sûr. Que est que vous voulez que je dire?" Jimmy asked with a perfect accent.

"Do you know what that means?"

"Sure, Mom. I said, what do you want me to say?"

Mom looked across the table to Dad and stared. Dad took a piece of bread and broke it in two.

"Son," he said, "what's the name of the new classmate of yours that came from Montreal?"

"Who do you mean, Dad?"

"Antoine, or something — something with an A."

"Ah, you mean Anthony. But he's from Kingston, Dad. Jamaica."

"I knew it was something Royal," Dad answered.

"Do you have any new friends that you haven't told us about," Mom said.

"Well, I do have a new friend," said Jimmy and hid his lower face in the napkin with the excuse of wiping his mouth. "His name is Francois."

Mom exhaled and smiled. Dad raised his fork, which meant *I told you so.*

✳ ✳ ✳

The days passed, and one afternoon, when Jimmy came in from playing outside, he pulled up his pants.

"Sweetie —have you been losing weight? Come here," Mom said and beckoned with her hand.

She took Jimmy by the belt and made the belt tighter, but she noticed one thing, the belt-hole that was raised as having been used for a long time was the one to the left.

"How about a nice piece of apple pie?" she asked.

He shook his head.

"Some cookies? I bought the maple ones you love."

"No, Mom. Thanks. We all have to do our part and tighten our belts a little."

"What do you mean? You don't have to tighten anything, young man. You've got to eat and grow."

"There's a time for everything," he said, "and now is a time for sacrifice. And no sacrifice is too big for *la liberté*."

"Listen," Mom said, and grabbed him by the wrists, "I don't know what your new friend has been telling you, but you don't have to make any sacrifices here. We're free. We have the Veterans to thank for that. We're not at war. Maybe Francois comes from a country where everything that he has been telling you is true, but you're safe here. You don't have to go hungry or suffer."

"Once you've lived through battle, *mon chére,* it never leaves you. You're always at war, in here," he tapped his forehead.

Mom didn't know how to answer. She let go of his wrists and stared into the wall for a long time.

* * *

When Dad came home from work that evening, Mom was waiting for him.

"How's work?" she asked, and before waiting for an answer, she said, "Have you shown Jimmy the old man's things?"

The old man meant Dad's great-grandfather. He had fought in a war a long time ago, and Dad had inherited a small box with some memorabilia.

"Job's fine," he said, "and nooooo. I haven't shown him anything. He's already obsessed with war as it is. He knows a lot more about it than I do."

"And what are you going to do about it?"

"Don't worry, I'll talk to him, take away his books."

"Which books?"

"He must have some books about the war, he wouldn't be so knowledgeable without them."

"Not at home, he doesn't."

"Do you think he's reading them at school?"

"I think this Francois is a bad influence for him. Must be a refugee from some war-torn country. He's telling him things."

"What kind of things?"

"What kind of things?"

"You know what," she said, "I want us to talk to the principal. I already made an appointment. It will be next Tuesday at noon"

* * *

That night, Dad waited until late before sneaking barefoot out of his room. He passed little Bettie's bedroom in the wood-panelled hall, checked on her and continued until he reached Jimmy's door. There was a whisper coming from the room.

He waited and listened. He caught a few words, here and there, *tue, mort,* but he couldn't understand their meaning. He took out his phone and opened the translator. On his screen, words and phrases appeared.

AND THEN THE BOCHE CLIMBED OVER THEIR TRENCHES, AND ONE OF OUR POILU'S OPENED FIRE WITH THE HOTCHKISS. WE THOUGHT WE WERE SAVED, BUT ARTILLERY SHELLS STARTED FALLING. I KNEW IT WAS ARTILLERY BY THE SOUND THEY MADE.

YOU COULD HEAR FAINT POPS, MUTED ENOUGH FOR YOU TO QUESTION IF YOU REALLY HEARD THEM. FIVE TO TEN SECONDS LATER, THE SHELLS WOULD COME. FIRST CAME THE WHISTLING SOUNDS LASTING A FEW SECONDS, LIKE CLOTH BEING RIPPED APART, WE KNEW WE DIDN'T HAVE TO WORRY ABOUT THOSE, THEY WOULD FALL MORE THAN A HUNDRED METERS BEHIND US.

THE NEXT ROUND, THE SHELLS FELL SHORT IN FRONT OF US, BUT STILL TOO FAR AWAY TO HURT US. THOSE FELT LIKE SLEDGEHAMMERS HITTING CORRUGATED STEEL, YOU'D HEAR A THUD AS THEY HIT THE GROUND, AND THEN A WAVE OF AIR AND SOUND WOULD PUNCH YOU.

THEY WERE CLOSING IN ON OUR POSITION, AND THE RIPPING NOISE BECAME SHORTER. IF A SHELL IS CLOSE ENOUGH TO HARM YOU, YOU'D ONLY HEAR IT FOR THE BRIEFEST OF TIMES, BUT AS CLEAR AS A BELL, AND THAT FRACTION OF A SECOND WOULD FEEL LIKE HOURS BECAUSE YOU KNEW IT WAS COMING FOR YOU.

WE COULD HEAR THE EXPLOSIONS GETTING NEARER, AND IMMEDIATELY AFTER EACH BLAST, WE HEARD WEIRD LITTLE SOUNDS ABOVE US. IT WAS THE

SHRAPNEL TUMBLING BREAKNECK THROUGH THE AIR…

Dad burst the door open, hoping to catch that Francois in Jimmy's room. Instead, he found Jimmy tucked in his bed, fast asleep, words coming from his lips in French.

"Wake up, wake up, son," he said and shook his boy awake. Jimmy opened his eyes and looked at his father. He had a vacant look in his eyes. "It was only a nightmare, don't worry, Jimmy, only a nightmare."

"War always is, Dad."

Dad held his son for five minutes in his arms and then searched the room for war books. He looked for half an hour without finding them and left the room without saying a word.

* * *

Mom was washing the plates Monday afternoon when Jimmy came in. Although her back was towards him, she detected something odd about the way he walked. From a look behind her shoulder, she could tell Jimmy was limping.

"Did you have fun in the playground, dear?" She asked.

"Sure, Mom."

She turned around and faced him. "Come give Mama a kiss, won't you?"

Jimmy did his best to act natural but dragged his left leg. She kissed him on the forehead and asked, "How did it happen?"

"How did what happen, Mom?"

"C'mon, let me see," she said and turned him around. His trousers had a large dark stain on the left buttock. She caressed the spot, and he winced. Her fingers came out bloodstained.

She crouched and lowered his pants. He had a jagged wound. "Who did this to you? How come the pants are not damaged, but you're bleeding? Did he ask you to take off your pants? Answer me."

"No, Mum," he murmured, "it was just shrapnel. Francois said that if he didn't take it out, it could get infected, and I could die."

"This is the last time you're seeing this Francois. Period. Am I clear?"

Jimmy muttered something.

"Am I clear?"

"It's not that easy, Mom," Jimmy said, "A man has to do what he has to do, even if it risks his life."

Mom slapped him hard enough to turn his head. Then she took her trembling hand to her mouth. "Oh, my God." A moment passed, and then her resolution returned. "Am I clear?"

"Yes, Mom."

* * *

On Tuesday, at noon, Mom and Dad had waited for the principal for forty-five minutes, when they were shown to his office.

There was a photo of the Pope behind his desk.

"To what do I owe the pleasure of your visit," the principal said and straightened his clerical collar.

They explained Jimmy's odd behaviour, his nightmares, their fears, but kept the wound to themselves.

"His knowledge of war is too," Mom struggled for words, "too firsthand to have been learned from books. That's not okay for a boy his age. We believe someone has been teaching him about war. Someone who has experienced it personally, someone who speaks French."

"I see," the principal said, "and from what I gather, you have someone in mind, don't you?" He reached for the intercom on his desk and said, "Violet, would you please call Madame DeVille? Tell her I want to see her immediately."

Mom and Dad looked puzzled.

"Madame DeVille," he said, "had a traumatic life before coming here to teach. But if she has been talking to the kids about what she went through in Africa, then I must stop it. Talking to kinder-gardeners about War for the love of God."

"Jimmy is in sixth grade," Mom said, "we were thinking about someone else, Francois, a schoolmate."

"Francois, you say," the principal said, and brought out a list of grade six students. He slid his finger down the list, and said, "He's not in grade six, maybe. . ." he grabbed the lists to the other grades and checked them. After going through all of them twice, he said, "We don't have anyone in the school with that name."

The intercom came to life. "Madame DeVille is here, sir. Should I send her in?"

The principal reflected for a couple of seconds and said, "Tell her I will talk to her afterwards, please. Tell her it's nothing bad, just. . . a misunderstanding."

Then he turned towards the parents and said, "If I were you, I'd figure out who this Francois is before he causes any more damage to your son." Then he opened the desk drawer, retrieved a small vial, and gave it to them. "Holy water," he said, "mark a cross on his forehead every night before he goes to sleep. He will feel the Lord's presence more physically with it."

As soon as they were outside the door to the office, Dad said, "I told you it was a bad idea. Catholic school, eh?"

* * *

From that day on, either Mom or Dad followed Jimmy on his way to and from school. Not right beside him, but far enough so they wouldn't be noticed. Not once did he stop to talk to anyone.

On Friday night, after dinner, Mom blocked Dad's exit from the bathroom. "If you won't do it, I'll do it," she said.

11

"I don't want my son to grow up believing in that sort of thing," he said, "Holy water," he chuckled. "I'm pretty sure it's just tap water, and besides, he hasn't spoken about Francois anymore."

"Don't," Mom said, "Tonight, I'll do it."

"I'll go with you," he said, "and you'll see it for yourself. It's not going to make a difference."

The night came, and both of them waited until the kids were fast asleep.

They tip-toed past little Bettie's room, and Dad crouched outside Jimmy's bedroom and pointed to his ear. Mom crouched beside him and listened. There was a murmur coming from the room. Dad brought out his phone and opened the translator. Mom pushed it down and whispered, "I studied French, I know what he's saying."

She eavesdropped, staring at the crack under the door. Sometimes she nodded; at others, she shook her head. Then she pressed a hand to her forehead and started crying.

"I can't stand it anymore," she said, "I'm going in."

She opened the door and knelt at the side of the bed, beside the whispering lips of her son. Out of her pocket, she brought the small vial the principal had given them. She opened the bottle and moistened her finger with it. As soon as she touched his son's forehead, a sort of vapor rose from him.

"Nous mourons tous, son heure viendra aussi", the vapor said.

"What did he say," Dad asked.

"We all die, his time will come too." Mom sobbed.

A Note

Thursday

You've made me jumpy, *extremely* jumpy. Five days ago, I opened the oven to check on my dinner, and I could swear I heard you whispering, "Meatloaf? Again?" Despite the oven's heat, a chill ran down my spine. "Leave me alone," I yelled, but you didn't answer.

Now I've realized that you can see what I'm doing, or you wouldn't have known about the meatloaf. That gave me the idea of writing to you. To tell you, I'm sorry for not being there for you, and to beg you to leave me alone. I hear your voice, see images, dream without being asleep. My friends say they are memories, part of mourning. What else can they be? But it's you. Please, just leave me alone.

Friday

Everything was dark when I went downstairs, and an image arose in my mind. You were right behind me, and I knew if I turned around, you'd open your mouth.

And through your open mouth, I would see the wall behind you, but not because you were a ghost, but because I could see through the hole you had blasted in your skull.

Why do you torture me so?

Saturday

I've been thinking, maybe I'm just jumpy because if *I* had committed suicide, I'd be raving mad against those who should have been there for me but weren't. I'd tear their chests open and rip their hearts out; I would crush their. . .

Where did that come from? What I'm feeling —it's not mine, though it feels as if it were. Am I feeling your feelings? Okay, I accept it, I'm terrified. Is that what you want?

Sunday

What you made me feel yesterday— it's stayed with me. You wouldn't have killed yourself if I had been here. How could I not see it coming? Was I that distant? God, what have I done? You know we needed the money, don't you? I wouldn't have agreed to travel as much if we didn't.

People always say, "We'll never know what she had to feel to do something like that," but I know. You made me experience it today: I feel like nothing is ever going to work for me, nothing *has* ever worked for me, meaning us, our family, our life, everything. There's no hope.

Monday

I went to the shrink today. There was nothing I could do, was there? I wasn't even in the same city as you. What could I have done? This couldn't have happened overnight, could it? I should've seen it coming, but how could I? There weren't any signs. You told me you were a little depressed, but aren't we all, sometimes? How could you kill yourself? How could you? If I'd known, I would've done something. Now it's too late, and I don't know what to do. We could've been so happy together.

Why are you laughing?

Tuesday

The last time I saw the clock, it read four am. I don't know for how long I've been awake; how many hours —or days. I need to move away from here. I don't want to sleep in the same bed I shared with you. I can't live in this house.

Wednesday

This is the last straw. Tonight, I didn't turn on the lights to go to the bathroom. The nightlight was enough. When I came back to bed, I saw a feminine shape over the sheets. It was your silhouette. Against the ebony headboard, as if projected on a sheer curtain, I could see your almond-shaped eyes. They were smiling with that malicious gaze— you were enjoying yourself.

I'm so tired of this. I reached out, but the only thing left was a cold spot. I heard laughter coming from the street. Your laughter. Who else is going to be outside my window at three am on a Wednesday night? Who else is going to have your laugh? You're toying with me. If you're coming for me, why wait? Why delay the inevitable? I shouldn't be saying this. I shouldn't even be thinking about it. But I believe you want me with you and you won't stop until you get what you want. Just like you did in life.

As long as I'm alive, you'll torture me.

I'm going to spare myself the pain.

Iris

I was walking home, following the route I took every day while Doug was alive. I missed him. I missed him a lot. Ever since the accident I've had the feeling of meeting him in the street. You know, looking at someone, and for a moment, *just for a moment* thinking it was him. I wished I could see him one more time.

So, I was walking past the little café by the park, where the willows are, when this guy bumps into me.

"Hi…Oops, sorry," he said. The order of the words was all wrong, but something in the way he talked stirred my curiosity.

"It's all good," I said, and was ready to keep walking when he spoke.

"Wait. What an amazing piece of trash!"

His finger was pointing at my locket. I gaped, shocked at what he had said. I was going to say something, but he was smiling. He smiled with almost infinite tenderness. I remembered Doug used to call my locket that: *amazing piece of trash.* He had crafted it himself, out of an old pocket-watch.

"Thank you," I replied with a shy smile.

"How about a cup of hot chocolate?" he said and winked.

"Sure," I said, but what I was really thinking was, *how does he know I love chocolate?* It wasn't the usual thing to ask. Guys always offered coffee first. When I'd say I didn't like coffee, they would ask, "tea then?" Not one asked for chocolate.

It was windy outside as November was almost upon us. I took hold of the lapels of my jacket. He extended his hand in front of me, like a gentleman of times past, pointing to the café's door.

I was feeling at the same time charmed by this new find, intrigued, and a little suspicious. Was it too good to be true?

We got to the counter, and he asked the barista for our drinks.

"What name should I write on your order?" said the man behind the counter.

"D," he answered. "Just D."

We went to a table by the window. My new acquaintance pulled out a chair for me to sit. Doug hated doing that. He would say, "Are you missing an arm or something?" He would only do it when he wanted to be especially nice to me. Doug knew I loved it.

We started talking about petty things like the weather and what I liked for lunch. That lasted for about half an hour. Next, we talked about my job and how I hated it.

"I want to do something with my life. It's just that I haven't decided exactly what," I said.

Then out of the blue, he said, "You've always been a storyteller, Iris. Just do it. Write."

I opened my mouth wide. My eyes must have bulged with surprise.

"How do you know I've always been a storyteller? Who told you my name is Iris?" I said as I started to get up from the chair. I hadn't given him my real name. How could he know? My hand was already touching the strap of my purse.

He stared at me, took my cup of chocolate, and turned it around so I could see what was written there. It read Iris.

"I don't remember giving my name to that guy," I said loudly. I pretended to be extremely angry, but the truth is, I was terrified. I didn't know what was happening. Was I going crazy? Then I remembered what he had said about me wanting to be a writer.

"How did you know I want to write?"

"Seriously?" he said and then pointed to my Idiot's Guide to Writing a Novel.

I breathed out.

"What are you afraid of?" he said.

"I — I feel like I've known you forever and — you seem to know me too well, and — I don't really know you."

"How do you know? I mean— how do you know, when you know someone?" he said.

"The time you spend with the other person, the things you share, the things you live through together. . ."

"You just feel it, don't you?" he said. "In the end, you just feel the intimacy, the trust, the sincerity —*love*."

I paused for a moment, feeling a knot in my throat. I didn't know what to say.

"Yes, you feel it," I said, and a tear came rolling down my cheek.

"And now you're feeling it, right?"

I nodded as I sniffed.

A song came up on the café's sound system. I'd heard it before, but I didn't know its name.

"I would really like to tell you how I feel, but I can't. That was the deal," he said.

"What deal? What are you talking about?"

He raised his finger to his mouth. "Shhh. Just listen. That's how I feel."

Then the music seemed to grow louder, and I listened.

I'll come back from death

Just to see you

So, you'd know that I love you still

Some loves are forever

And ours is like that

And I want you to kiss me right now.

Then we both lifted from our seats, and stood up, locking eyes. We took the step that separated us and embraced.

We kissed, closing our eyes, and for a brief moment, our souls fused.

I lost track of time. The kiss ended, and when I opened my eyes, his eyes were on mine. They were like a dam about to burst. Then he lip-sung the ending.

I don't want to leave you

(though)

I don't want to leave you

(though)

I don't want to leave

But I must.

We embraced harder. Then he looked me straight in the eyes, a tear flowing down his cheek.

"Be happy," he said, "Do it for me." His voice was breaking.

I nodded and saw his lip trembling.

I closed my eyes to kiss him goodbye. When I opened them, he had gone.

Bad Publicity

I have to use the washroom. I have to. It's late, and the only establishment open is the Mermaid Café. I see the green and white logo shining from the other side of the parking lot, beckoning.

I don't even think about it. I just walk as fast as I can through the empty parking spots. I can't run anymore. If I do, I will pee myself.

I open the crystal door with the mermaid logo, and a bell sings announcing my arrival. From the granite counter, the green-aproned barista faces a customer and says, "I'm sorry, Ma'am, but as I've told you, we're not allowed to let the customers use the washroom after dark."

"What kind of stupid rule is that?" Says a middle-aged woman with a scarf on her head.

"Company policy, Ma'am. I'm sorry."

"But the key is right there. I could have just taken it," the middle-aged woman says and hits the hanging key, which starts swinging in the arc it has scratched on the wall.

"I would have chased you for it," the barista says. "Believe me, you don't want to go into that washroom after dark."

I frown at the oddness of the comment. *What can she possibly mean?*

"Go to hell. I'm never coming here again," the customer says and exits the café, slamming the door behind her. The glass enclosure of the café vibrates.

My legs are crossed, I'd pee otherwise. I'm determined. I won't ask for the key.

"A Triple-Whipped Macchiato and a grilled turkey sandwich, hot please," I say, hoping that combination will take her the longest time to prepare. She types my order into the computer. She takes ages, or so it seems to me. I can't hold it anymore. I finally pay, and as soon as she turns around, I steal the key.

I tiptoe as fast as I can to the back of the Café and find the door to the washroom. Right beside the doorknob, a red rectangle with white letters reads, "WARNING: DO NOT OPEN DOOR AFTER DUSK."

Fuck policies, I mutter and insert the key in the lock. It turns. I hear the barista calling me. I shut the door and lock it. I don't care if they arrest me afterward, I'm using this toilet.

Pleasure rises through me as I relieve myself. I let out a big sigh. Then I hear it. There's another sigh, just following mine. I look around. There's no one in the small room besides me. I see the hand dryer, the basin, the mirror, even the motion sensor for the lights, but there's not a single place from where the sound could have drifted.

Then it comes again — a deeper sigh.

Good God! Someone's having sex in the other washroom.

Then I realize there isn't another room next to it. This toilet is the only one in the Café. The muted sound of the blender comes faintly from the door. *How come I can hear the sighs clearly but not the blender?*

Another sigh comes and a moan. Then labored breathing joins the moaning.

I hear a woman's voice right beside my ear, "Gentle. You're being too rough."

The labored breathing gets faster.

"Stop. You're hurting me!" the voice says.

There's a sound as if someone's head is banging against the wall.

"Stop!"

The voice sounds desperate.

Then the lights of the washroom turn off. The room becomes as dark as if I had plunged into crude oil. I wave my arms at the sensor to make the lights turn on again. As soon as I start swinging them, I have the certainty that if I continue, I'll touch the two sweaty bodies beside me. I stop. My rational mind tells me I'm by myself. I've seen the room with the lights on, but I *know* I'm not alone.

"No, No, No, NO," she shrieks. I hug myself as she screams. I hear the wet sounds of someone repeatedly pounding something. She is sobbing now. No more yelling.

"Please don't," the voice says. "Don't kill me."

It cackles. I don't hear her anymore.

The labored breathing comes closer to me. I can hear it right beside my neck. I recoil and fall from the toilet. My hands touch something wet and viscous on the floor. I think of all the filth on the washroom floor, but then it dawns on me: *It feels like blood.*

I'm pushing myself against the wall when the lights come back on. I hear voices coming very faintly from beneath the door. Someone's placing an order for a Cappuccino. I stand up, fearful that the lights will turn off again, but nothing happens. From where I am, I can see myself in the mirror. I expect my clothes to be full of blood, or urine at least, but there's nothing on them. The floor is clean too.

I race for the doorknob. *Oh God, it's going to be jammed. I'm going to be stuck here forever.* I turn the handle, and the door opens. I am free. I want to cry, and my whole body quivers. I don't want anyone to think what I believe about myself: *She's beyond help now, she's raving mad.* I tense my muscles. I walk to the counter, return the key, and rush out of the café.

TV

When people call to cancel their TV service, ninety times out of a hundred, it's because our competition has brainwashed them into believing their service is better. It's not, okay? Who has bundles like ours?—but I'm getting sidetracked here. What I'm trying to tell you, is that only ten percent of our clients actually want to cancel their TV service.

Nine out of those ten, want to watch everything online. Those subscribers don't need any TV channels as such, so we offer them a streaming package, and they end up staying with us. But every once in a while, you get a case where they genuinely don't want anything to do with the TV. They're not canceling to go to somcone else. They're not sticking to streaming. They just don't want anything to do with technology, not today, not ever again.

Usually, that lone individual is the head of a family, who's had a religious conversion to one of those sects, where they don't allow technology—you know what I'm talking about, don't you?

But when I received that call, I knew something was off.

"Okay, sir. If you don't want the service, I'll cancel it for you, but you have to return the following items: PVR, Home Theater, SmartScreen..."

"I'm not going back in there," he interrupted.

"Beg your pardon?"

"I said, I'm not going back in there."

I waited for a moment trying to figure out what he was referring to.

"If you don't want to bring it to our offices. . ." I began but was cut short.

"I won't go back into that house. Period. You pick it up."

"I'm afraid that's not possible, sir."

"Sue me, then." He said. His tone was adamant.

"Let me speak to my supervisor, Sir. Just one moment."

I spoke to my manager. She told me we could pick up the equipment from the man's house, but the penalty would be stiff.

"That's okay," the client said," even if you had tripled the penalty, I would have considered it cheap. You'll find the key under the entrance mat." He hung up.

What I didn't know then, was that I would personally have to pick up the equipment, and on top of that, it would have to be after my shift.

I took the company's van to the address on the work order. The house looked just like any other house on the block: sloping roof with dormers, small front porch, white grilled windows, white gutters breaking the tidy lines of the house, trash cans beside the automatic garage door.

The only difference was that most houses on that block had at least one car parked on the driveway. This house had none, so I parked on it. The sun had just set over the roofs behind me.

I picked up the key. It was precisely where the client had told me it would be. I opened the door, and as I stepped inside the lights turned on by themselves. I didn't want anyone to think I was trespassing, so I bellowed, "Hello, is there somebody here?"

No one answered, but it felt as if there was someone in the house. I tried again, "Hello. I'm from the TV Company. Anyone there?"

It still felt as if there was someone in the house. I can't explain why. Homes with no one in them sound—

hollow, echoing more than they do when there's someone in the house. Also, there's always the little noises that betray even the quietest person.

One of those sounds, a click, came from the kitchen.

Apparently, someone had left while the coffee machine brewed a Cappuccino. The device was still trying to rid itself of the plastic cup. Each attempt was a click. I removed the plastic container, and the coffee poured into a mug. I touched the coffee. It was cold. What would make you leave in such haste? Maybe he had to fly somewhere far away, as fast as he could, just like when they told me my Mom was in the hospital, dying. But wouldn't his wife or neighbors, look after the house? Had no one been here? Maybe he was single.

I turned around and saw the photos on the wall. There was a man that appeared in most of the pictures, which I guessed was our client. The man had a young blond woman with him. Hmmm, weird.

I was there to do a job, I thought, so I might as well get it done.

If the home theater wasn't in the living room, then in my experience, it would be either in the master bedroom or in the basement. Logic told me to check the basement first. Through the windows I saw that night had settled outside. It must have been a moonless night because it was extremely dark.

I got to the stairs and hit the light switch. The lights wouldn't go on. As dark as it was outside, the stairs going down, looked darker. I didn't feel like going down, so I walked up to the master bedroom.

It wasn't tidy. The bed was unmade, and clothes were scattered over it, women's clothes on one side, and men's on the other. I walked around the bed. An open suitcase was abandoned on the floor, a cream-colored blouse lying on top of it.

My theory about the emergency call in the middle of the night was gathering momentum. I had found evidence. I took the work order from my back pocket. I had to pick up a PVR from another TV. Most people have them in their bedrooms. I looked around and found the TV. It was flat on top of the dresser, the screen facing the drawers instead of the bed as it should have.

"And my wife says I'm weird," I blurted.

I heard voices coming from below. Oh Shit! I had to look as if I was working. I disconnected the PVR and wrapped the cables around it.

"Hello, is there someone here?" I said as I walked down the stairs, the PVR tucked in my armpit. The voices came from the basement, and they were having a passionate conversation.

"I love you, Liana," the man said.

"But I'm married," she said.

"I don't care; let's run away. Let's do it right now."

Then the voices were cut short by a jingle and a voice advertising an insurance company. It was a soap opera. The lights to the basement-stairs were on now. Someone was watching the TV.

The light from the stairs barely spilled into a large entertainment room, which was dark. The only other light in the room besides the one coming from the stairs was that of the TV. I expected to see someone sitting on the fake leather couches, but I couldn't see anyone.

"Hello," I said. No one replied.

I turned on the lights. The room was empty. There was a sizeable rust-colored stain on the floor, between the sofa and the TV. Someone must have spilled a full bottle of hot sauce by the looks of it. I went to sit on one of the couches.

"Oh God, this is what I call a Rec room," I said. I rarely speak out loud when I'm by myself, but I felt the need to do it. My grandma told me to whistle if I was scared. Talking to myself felt like whistling. "If I spent all my paycheck I could probably get one of these. . . The wife would kill me, though."

I got up, *unplugged* the TV, the PVR, and the speakers. I was wrapping the cables when I noticed that my breath showed, as if it was freezing. It had been warm just a moment ago. I felt —someone— in the room. Goosebumps erupted throughout my body as the dread chilled me. I knew that if I dared to look, I would find someone there, watching me.

I steeled myself and turned around. Electricity ran up to through my spine. The room was empty. Stuttering, I managed to ask, "He-He-He-Hello. Is there someone here?"

Little more than a whisper came from the TV. "There is."

I yelled as I run from the house, knowing that if I stayed, that thing would get me, and no one would ever hear from me again.

I got out, not even bothering to close the door after me. I took the van to the nearest Best Buy. I maxed out my credit cards and bought a home theater just like the one in the house. It was the only way I could return the equipment to the company. My boss wasn't going to believe me. It was either that or resigning. I'm not rich; I need the money. I'm selling my own TVs in case you're interested. I don't even know what I'm going to tell my wife, but I'm not going back into that house *ever* again.

Dyaree

Dec 24th- My Mommy is mean, Daddy too. I'm grounded, and I have nothing to do. Mommy said if I keep imagining things I might as well write them down. She says it's called a Dyaree. I'm not imagining things. I don't know why they are so mad.

Dec 25th- Cristmass. I got a huge Teddy bear, just like the one I wanted. My little brother Tommy got a train. Today at breakfast, Mommy made my favorite pancakes. She told me she loved me. I love it when she touches my hair. I guess we were all just tired yesterday. Moving to another house is hard work. I still have to stay in my room. We'll see what Daddy says when he gets back.

Dec 26th- Mommy called me a liar. She yelled at me. Told me to shut up. Daddy had to make *her* shut up. She cried. Daddy asked me to describe the man I had seen. He told me people don't dress like that anymore. He asked me if I had seen it in a book or a movie. I told him the man by the stair dresses like that. Then Daddy got mad too and told me there is no one else in the house. I'm going to stop writing. My tears are [unreadable] the paper.

Dec 26th- Later. I saw him again. My door opened. I thought it was Mommy checking on me. He came into the room and took off his hat. He put it on the boxes by my bed. He smiled. I screamed. Daddy came running. The man went into the closet. Daddy searched, but he couldn't find him. I said I'm not a liar, and I pointed to the hat, but the hat was gone. He told me it was just a nightmare. Was it?

Dec 27th- I think my Mommy is the liar. I think she sees him too. She was cooking today while I was playing with Teddy on the kitchen floor. The man walked in. My Mommy and I both turned at the same time. Mommy dropped the pot. She said I distracted her. Maybe I am a bad girl.

Later. My Mommy told Daddy she had dropped the pot because of me. He made me promise not to speak of my imaginary friend anymore. I told Daddy the man is not my friend, and that he is real. Daddy sent me to bed without supper. I shouldn't have said anything.

Dec 28th- Something really bad happened today. Tommy was taking a bath in the tub while Mommy was drying my hair. I turned to the tub, and I saw the man. He was in the bathtub, where Tommy should have been. My Mommy threw the electric drier into the tub. Everything went dark. Daddy said that it blew the breaker. He says Tommy will be just fine. I'm not so sure.

Dec 29th- Tommy is not feeling very well today. He tosses a lot in bed. Daddy is taking care of him. My Mommy hasn't come out of her room all day. I can hear her crying. She says she doesn't want to live anymore. She told Daddy she was a monster. Why does she think she is the monster? The man is the monster, isn't he? I am a bad girl. I should have never told her about the man.

Later. Mommy came out of her room at last. She sat on Tommy's bed with Daddy. I could see them from my room. After a little while, Daddy had to go to the washroom. Mommy couldn't stop looking at the floor. The man must have been waiting. He took Tommy's blankie and made a bundle. It really looked as if Tommy was in it. Mommy kept staring at the floor until the man laughed. She looked at him, and her eyes almost came out. She said, "don't you dare," just as he stepped out of the room. He ran to the stairs. Mommy chased him. Mommy fell. I screamed. Why do I keep crying?

Even later. I hope Mommy is okay. Daddy told me not to look down the stairs. I have to take care of Tommy while he goes for help. He told me to pack. We're going to start the year somewhere else. There I won't see that man anymore. I hear the door to my room opening. I hope it's Daddy. . .

Stink

March 16th, 1994

Dear son:

I've always been honest with you about what my life was before I straightened my ways and became respectable. I don't know if you're proud of me, but I've tried to be someone you could look up to. I know my time is near, so I want to tell you how proud I am of you. You've always been the one with whom I could be the most honest, but there's one tale that I haven't told you. The story of why I left that life, and why I know my end is near. It has to do with what you smelled here the other day.

Back during the war, the Army needed a shipment for the war in Europe, so we had to fill the guts of three ten-thousand ton ships with tinned fish. We had toiled at the sea-side cannery for three whole days without rest. The delivery was so large that the warehouse on the bottom floor was already full.

"Hey boss, where do we put the extra crates," I shouted at the foreman.

The foreman placed the pencil he was writing with on his ear and yawned. "How many more are there?"

"Ten more just like this one," I said, patting a box as tall as me and just as long.

"Set them on the main floor," the foreman said, "set the first five, and then check to see if the clearance is good enough to have the other ones on top."

"Yes, sir," I said, and after checking that the height was right, we did as he had ordered. The wooden floor had first roared, then creaked with the weight, but eventually, the grumbling had stopped.

I rested my head against one of the crates and dozed off. The foreman startled me by shaking my shoulder.

"I'm giving everyone the day off. Get in line for your money," he said and almost poked my nose with his index finger, "Close the trapdoor beside your bunk before you leave, and make sure all the pulleys are stowed. I want you back here tomorrow, seven a.m. sharp, you hear me? I can still make fish-food out of you."

Now, for almost anyone, fish-food would be a metaphor, but the scuttlebutt was that he had actually tied a man to one of the stilts that supported the cannery over the water. Usually, that would only be gentle torture, but with all the fishes' blood and guts, there were sharks in those waters, shallow as they were.

 I retrieved my wages and walked up the plank toward firm land.

"Hey Rooster," someone called from the street. I looked up and saw my friend Stinky already coming back to the cannery. He carried two gallons of liquor under each armpit, and another two in his hands. He was smiling as he did only on pay-days, smiling like a kid with a new toy.

Booze at the cannery was tolerated on the off days, as long as we were sober for work the next day. I don't know if the ladies would have been allowed in the cannery or not, but they stayed far away from it. They complained it stank. Actually, the ladies wouldn't get near us until after we'd had a bath, which was fine as it was included in the price.

"Heading for the ladies?" Stinky asked.

"Yep and I see that you've got yourself some company," I said and pointed at all the alcohol he was carrying.

"That right, mister. That's all the company I want for now. The love of my life, they are." Stinky said, and craned his neck to kiss the bottle under his armpit but couldn't. "Wanna join me?"

"Maybe later, Stinky," I said and patted him gently on the shoulder so he wouldn't drop any of the bottles. He was a good friend and drunk as he might be, he always knew everything that happened in the cannery.

Since Stinky preferred booze to ladies, he rarely took a bath. That's what gave him his nickname.

I was so damn tired that I fell asleep in the whorehouse, and didn't return to the cannery on time. I sneaked in, fearing the foreman would tie me to the stilts as he has promised. I expected to find the men working noisily as always, but the only thing I could hear was the men's shuffling feet scrubbing the planks and the drone of some machines. Something felt wrong. Behind those noises there was a silence as if I had entered a church.

Stinky would surely tell me what was happening. I went to see the board where our shifts were registered. We both had the morning shift off. That meant that he would be in the attic, where we slept.

The garret was dead silent. I went to Stinky's bed, but he wasn't there. I looked about dead saw him in a shadowy corner on the side closest to the open sea. He was combing his greasy hair.

"Hi Stinky. Everything all right?"

He shook his head and pushed out his chin, pointing at something. Jeez! I had left the trap-door open beside my bunk, and the seagulls crying was louder because of it. I hurried to close it.

"Why is everyone so quiet? Did he finally tie someone to the stilts?" I asked.

He shook his head, "Worse. You gotta see it yourself."

"Is it worth looking at?" I was still dog-tired and didn't feel like doing anything.

A moment passed without an answer.

"Well, is it?" I asked and started taking my boots off.

He shrugged. "Soon after you see me again, you'll die," he said.

He didn't sound drunk, but he rarely did.

"You gotta stop drinking, Stinky."

"*Now* you tell me," He said and chuckled.

I drifted off to sleep.

Sometime later, I awoke to the sound of hammering very close by. The trap-door was being nailed shut. I knew something was wrong. I rushed in my socks to the main floor, where the big shipment had been stored. Only a jagged hole remained. Through the shattered boards, I saw the sea crashing into the stilts.

"It happened last night," the foreman said, "Stinky was as drunk as always, and he fell on top of the shipment. His weight brought everything down."

"But I saw him this morning!"

"Can't be. The sharks got him. They," the foreman started, but couldn't speak another word. He kept looking down, shaking his head, sniffing violently.

That very day I stopped drinking, womanizing and gambling. Eventually, I saved enough to put me through college. The rest is history, and you know everything there is to know.

There's something else I need to tell you.

All of my life I felt guilty about Stinky. I really can't remember if I closed the trapdoor or not. For years I had nightmares in which he would come to take me away. When anyone spoke of death coming for anyone, I always thought of him.

Stinky said he'd come back for me, remember? When you came to visit me and mentioned the smell, I didn't have the guts to tell you. Several times recently, I think I've seen Stinky, but my senses are not that sharp anymore, so I had my doubts. Now I can't deny it—you smelled him too. It's my time, son.

I'm proud of you,

Dad.

Social Media

That night while I brushed my teeth, the temptation came — once again — to check my social media. My phone vibrated every time I got a new message, and I hadn't felt it shudder, but since I started having these dreams about two weeks ago, I had to check. I felt that if I didn't check it often enough, something terrible would happen.

I have this sensation, this certainty. . . it's like when you have to check all the stove's valves five times before leaving or inspect the doors' locks precisely seven times, because if you don't — something horrible, it's going to happen. It isn't something concrete; it's just this sense of impending doom.

As I was saying, that night, I unlocked my phone only to discover that there was nothing new on it, but while I was holding it, it shook, and a little round bubble with the number one appeared.

You have a new message from Jules DeGrancy.

Damn hackers, I thought immediately. It had to be hackers. Who else would do such a thing? It couldn't be Jules.

One dream arose from my memory. It was nighttime, I was in my bedroom sleeping on top of the quilt fully dressed. The phone was ringing, I could see it screen down on the nightstand. I knew it was Jules, but I didn't want to answer. The phone kept ringing, I turned it around and confirmed it was Jules calling, but I didn't want to answer, because…

My friend Jules had been dead for seven years.

The anniversary of his death was due in a couple of weeks. Maybe Norah, his widow, was using his account to organize something with his contacts. That sounded reasonable, but she would've told me. My hand trembled a little as I opened the message.

Hey Mat. I need to talk to you.

My mouth was dry, and it was hard to swallow. I typed back: Who are you?

What do you mean? I'm Jules.

I'm reporting you, I typed, and closed the message.

I stopped smoking ten years ago, but somehow I found a pack in one of my old caches. The cigarette tasted like a tarmac on a hot day, but I needed it. I contacted the social media company and told them what had happened. They informed me that only the next of kin would be able to close the account.

I didn't want to open old wounds, but this had to stop. I had to contact Norah. Why would someone pretend to be him? Would they ask me for something? Deep down, a thought pushed itself into my mind. What if it *is* Jules.

I took out my phone and called Norah.

"Hi, it's me," I said.

"Finally," she said, "why didn't you call me back?"

"I couldn't. It's too much."

"We are lonely Mat, and we're perfect for each other."

"It's not going to happen again," I said.

"But why? It's not like you didn't enjoy it."

"But he was my best friend."

She chuckled, and I could imagine her shaking her head.

"That's what you say, but you keep coming back for more," she said.

Silence.

"I know," I said, "you're right, but I keep having these dreams. . ."

"Don't start with that, okay? Why don't we go somewhere nice for the weekend?"

I didn't answer immediately. I struggled to find the best way to tell her about the message and about what I was feeling.

"Look, I have to go," she said. "Call me before Thursday, okay? Bye."

I said "Bye" and hung up. She wasn't going to believe me about the messages. Not even if I showed them to her. Maybe it was just guilt. Why was I thinking about Jules so much? What would I feel if my best friend — never mind. I wouldn't feel anything, I would be dead. But the messages were real. Who could be sending them?

The next day on an elevator, a man stole a glance at me, his expression told me he thought I was crazy. I don't blame him. I had checked my phone eighth times in four floors, my hands wouldn't stop shaking, and any noise made me swerve in fear.

I bought a brand new packet of cigarettes.

After supper, I made a resolution: I wasn't going to tell Norah about the messages. I would solve my issues and take her to the Spa Hotel in the mountains that she has been telling me about.

If a hacker had breached his account's security, then another hacker would be able to close his account. If Jules had been alive, I would have gone directly to him. He was the best hacker I've ever seen. He hacked the university servers to prove he could have straight A's if he wanted to. He changed all his grades and even printed a report card as a souvenir. Immediately afterwards, he returned his grades to what they had been. I felt nostalgic. I missed my good, old, rule-bending, you-wont-stop-me, friend.

After I made the reservation for the Spa and told Norah about it, I spent the rest of my evening trying to figure out how to hire a hacker. At last, I found one and left him a message with my contact info. By then, my shaking had spread to both hands. I stank of nicotine. I wouldn't be able to sleep if I didn't have one last smoke — and a Scotch.

I was dosing off when I felt a vibration in my pocket. I reached out for my phone, but my pocket was empty. My phone was on the nightstand. I had started to get these "phantom calls" a couple of weeks back. My doctor said most people with a smartphone have them. While I had my hand in my pocket, I felt a vibration again, and then, less than a second afterward, my phone shook, and a new message appeared.

Are you mad at me? Why aren't you answering?

The Scotch made me daring. I was fed up with being afraid. I decided to play along. Probably it was just a damn teenager trying to squeeze some money out of me.

I haven't heard anything from you in the last seven years, and you expect me not to be upset? I typed.

It hasn't been that long, has it? It's been a rough couple of weeks since everything went fubar with the car.

Fubar. Shivers ran from my waist to my neck. Who uses "fubar" nowadays? No one. Only a WWII buff like Jules. The impersonator was good. But of course, he had Jules's social media information to know which words he used, what he liked, who his friends were—everything.

Everything.

I poured some more Scotch into the glass and drank it straight.

What do you want? I wrote.

To talk to you. Don't you want to talk to me anymore?

Okay. I'm listening.

Whoa. I thought you of all people would be more interested in knowing what lies beyond the great unknown.

Meaning?

C'mon. Don't you remember that conversation we had on that fishing trip? You had always wanted to know what happened after death.

The whiskey glass slipped from my grasp, as a frozen clamp crushed my heart. If I remembered correctly, we were alone in that boat. The shaking worsened. Had I ever talked about it to anyone else? We were in the middle of the lake. There was no one. How could he know? I closed the chat and lit another smoke.

I realized something. Who knows when the microphone on our phones is on? Or the camera? For all I know, someone might be recording us all the time. But to what purpose? Neither Jules nor I worked in anything worth spying on. It made no sense. Probably we were off the grid on that lake. I was cold and turned to grab my sweater. I felt a vibration in my thigh and knew my phone would start in a second if I let it, so I turned it off.

In the morning, the hacker called me on my landline to set up an appointment.

That evening, I was in a basement room with black garbage bags taped to the windows as blackout. I sat next to what looked like puke-stained office chairs. A bare lightbulb shone from the ceiling, but no less than six monitors illuminated the hacker's face. He had neglected the décor, but the technology was state-of-the-art. Smoke rose from a lit but forgotten cigarette in my hand.

"We'll be in, in no time," the hacker said. He tapped the keyboard at a steady pace and pressed the Enter key after each burst of typing. It seemed to me his tempo was getting progressively faster. Then he hit the Enter key with particular emphasis. My pulse throbbed on my neck.

"Is it ready? Is it closed?" I asked.

"Who are we messing with?" he said, "Whoever it is, he's blocking our attempts," the hacker said.

Between each line of code, a single sentence repeated itself.

Why do you want to shut me off?

I took a drag. It couldn't be Jules. Could it?

The hacker kept trying for another half-an-hour, but he was getting nowhere. My head throbbed in sync with my heart. I was out of breath. I felt as if I had run a race and lost. I had an idea.

"Can you know where he is physically located?" I asked, already imagining a pair of thugs getting hold of him.

The hacker typed, paused, typed again, paused, typed a third time, and asked, "Who the hell are we messing with? I've never seen anyone do this."

"Why?" I asked.

"Because according to these — his open hand pointed to the screens— the person blocking our attempts is in this room…"

Deep down, I knew. I stared at the screens, trying to find an explanation, but something caught my eye. Through the cigarette smoke, I could see Jules' diaphanous head and hands. He was typing. Then Jules raised his head and looked at me. He pointed at a monitor.

In the middle of the screen, four words shone back at me.

I KNOW ABOUT NORAH.

All the oxygen left the room, and I gasped suffocating as my head exploded. I felt faint. I looked around the room for an explanation, gasping for air. Everything swirled around me. I heard the hacker's voice coming from far, far away, calling my name while I collapsed to the floor.

Mama

My patient sat on the couch as usual, and immediately said, "My mother died a couple of years ago, around Mother's Day." Then he went silent. His knee seesawed as he fidgeted with a pen.

"She was a difficult woman, to say the least. I'm not going to speak ill of the dead, but I'm not going to lie to you either. She lived her last years in a third world country: warm winters, unhurried life…"

"Which country was it?" I said, but he ignored the question.

"She wasn't that far from us, just a flight away really, but neither my siblings nor I visited her often. I can say I was caught up in my work and my responsibilities. I can blame it on the kids or my wife. But the truth is, we honestly didn't want to visit."

He fell silent for a while. I prodded him on. "Was there a particular reason?"

"When we visited, she always did something that made us leave early. One time I heard her yelling at my kids,

'I'm not letting you out of there until you learn where to pee.' She had locked them in the bathroom for wetting their beds. We had to fight her for the key to let them out."

"Did your kids wet their beds often?" I asked.

"They never had accidents at home. Only when we visited her, and the things she would…"

My patient shook his head several times, then stopped but said nothing more. On and off, he shook his head in silence for a while.

"If you don't talk to me, there's nothing I can do to help you," I said.

"I did say I wasn't going to speak ill of the dead, didn't I."

"You can say anything here. Don't judge yourself. Just let it out. Did anyone else visit her?"

"No, something similar happened to her friends. When she decided to move there, she told us she was going with one of her friends, a widower too. I was glad. I thought she would have company that way. But three months later, her friend was gone. Enough said."

"So she was alone then?"

"She had visitors on and off, but most of the time she was by herself, yes. I guess it was a peaceful life, or maybe not. She got a gardener jailed for stealing her azaleas. I checked the photos of her property, and I couldn't find azaleas. As far as I know, she never had any. That's just a fact, I'm not judging her."

"How do you feel about her being alone?"

He shrugged. "Sorry, I guess. I'm telling you all this so that you understand that when my mother died in a car accident, it was only me who decided to go to the island and prepare everything for her funeral. I had to fly in as soon as I learned of her demise."

"Didn't you have conflicting thoughts, one part of you wishing to go, but the other…"

"I had to go. I was her executor, and by law, the burial has to take place within forty-eight hours from the time of death. It's hot, and they don't embalm the bodies so…"

I nodded. "I thought they embalmed bodies everywhere nowadays,"

"Well, they don't, and they keep some very peculiar traditions. They don't allow cremation of the bodies, for instance, and I had to keep vigil over her body during the night, to make sure she was dead, and not in a cataleptic fit."

"What about confirmation from medical equipment?"

My patient half-laughed, and shrugged, "What can I say? I was left alone in the mortuary with her. It was a big, high-ceilinged building with grey marble floors. All the windows were blacked out, and it smelled of decaying flowers.

There weren't a lot of other people mourning their dead that night. Maybe not a lot of people had died, or perhaps the mortuary was always like this: desolate.

The first four hours or so, I sat diligently on a stuffed black chair next to her plain wooden coffin. After midnight, all the noises in the building died down. I felt drained: the call telling me of her passing, the rush to get there on time, dealing with my emotions. . . Therefore, I rested my head on one of the couches by the door and was asleep before I knew it.

A child's crying woke me up.

I heard sobbing nearby. It seemed—I'll never find the words. I'll say it sounded forlorn. I stood up and followed the sound. I walked out of my mother's wake room and into the main hall of the mortuary. The sobbing reverberated on the white marble walls. The light of the moon filtered from a skylight.

The sound came from the wake room across the hall. My footsteps echoed as I walked toward it. I stopped at the door and peeked. There was a coffin, and beside it, a child on the floor holding her knees with her arms. It was a girl. There was nobody else in the room.

"Hola," I said, "¿necesitas ayuda?"

She kept staring at the floor.

"Niña, ¿estas bien?" I struggled with my Spanish. I wanted to ask her where her parents were.

"¿Donde está tu papá o mamá?"

The little girl glanced at the coffin and howled with pain. She muttered something. I only distinguished one word: Mama.

"Ven, ven," I said, motioning with my hand for her to come. Her shoulders trembled with her sobs.

"Vamos, ven," I said, offering my hands to pick her up, but she didn't respond.

I ran down the stairs and knocked like a madman on the night manager's office. Through the window, I could see him fast asleep over the desk. The glass of the window rattled with each knock, but he didn't stir. Then I jerked the lock on the door, and he woke up.

In my anxiety, I forgot about talking in Spanish.

I did my best to explain the situation. Seemingly, he couldn't understand my meaning, but his English was perfect.

After four times of retelling the story I grabbed him by the shirt and said, "If you don't come down there with me right now, I'm going to drag you there. She shouldn't be there alone. "

"Okay, okay, calm down. I'll go with you."

He walked with me to the wake rooms. I thought I would feel better being with someone else, but the echoes from the walls singled out our steps, making me feel just as lonely.

"This is your mother's wake room," he said, pointing at my mother's room, "and this is the room of your sister."

He showed me the room where I had seen the girl.

"What do you mean?"

"Your mother had adopted a child —I thought you knew—and she died in the accident with her. The girl's coffin is in there."

I looked him in the eyes and saw he told the truth.

I imagined my mother as a wonderful mom to this girl who was in ruins for losing her. I saw Mother waking up from death to care for her child crying in the night. Then the penny dropped. That wasn't even a realistic possibility.

I ran. I escaped into the dark streets and dashed among closed street food shops. Stray dogs rummaged through the garbage on the floor. The streetlamps half-heartedly illuminated diffused circles on the asphalt. The rest was saffron-tinged darkness. Someone far away laughed drunkenly. As I ran, I kept looking back… looking back.

"What did you expect to find?" I said and saw my patient struggle for words.

"I don't know."

He became silent again, so I asked. "Why did you run?"

"I wasn't frightened I had seen the girl's ghost. But — if ghosts existed, I wasn't going to wait to see Mom's. You don't know what she's capable of."

Instrumental Relationship

"I don't care, doctor. I want my father medicated," the woman said.

"Well, then I'm sorry but you're going to need another psychiatrist to do it. The only things that make you believe your father is crazy is that he doesn't want to speak with anyone, and that he plays the cello nonstop."

The woman swiped a strand of hair from her face. They were outside the room where her father was playing. The door was open, and music was pouring from the opening.

"Look at him! See how he's moving his lips," the woman cried. "He's saying something — to someone. Someone we can't *see!*"

"I can see his lips moving, but we don't have any way of knowing if he's talking with someone, or if he's talking to himself," the doctor said. "You two have just had an important loss. In time, he'll assimilate it."

She was about to respond when he continued.

"Look, your father spent more than forty years with your mother —that's more time than a child spends with her parents. That creates a bond, *mighty difficult* to break. Her passing is very hard on him."

"I don't doubt it, but he's not taking it right. Look at him. There he goes again — I'm sure he has — how do you call it?" She snapped her fingers, trying to recall the word.

"Objectum-sexuality?" the doctor said. "Look now, your father had an undeniable partner, and believe me; it wasn't that cello."

* * *

The old man got up with his cane, and swaying, approached the chair in which the cello was resting. He took the instrument and used it as support. The cane echoed in the room as it fell and bounced on the wooden floor. He had done it on purpose. He would pick it up later when he needed to stand.

He placed the cello between his legs and sat down. He caressed the smooth varnish of the instrument, following the tiger-like vein of the wood. By the movement alone, anyone would have thought about the caress given to a loved one. The curves of the instrument and the place at the waist of the cello, where the old man had placed his hand, reinforced the image.

He adjusted the cello and took the neck of the instrument. He placed his fingers on the strings as if he was stroking the hair in his beloved's nape. Then he grazed the strings with the bow.

A prodigious sound flowed from the instrument. Anyone would've taken it for a feminine voice, anyone open to listening.

The old man touched his head to that of the instrument and tenderly rested his white-grey hair against the cello. He closed his legs, holding the instrument, and started swaying, as if they were dancing.

The bow gave off white particles of resin, while he rubbed it against the strings.

The light seeped into the room, through the ajar shutters of the window, creating light beams in the darkness. Beams that fell at the base of the instrument, illuminating it. In this light, the old man appeared young again, like he did when he met his beloved.

"Thank you for staying with me, my darling. Thank you for doing it like this. . ." the old man said without emitting a single sound. Only his lips moved.

Suddenly a gust of wind entered the room and swirled the air around the cello. The particles suspended in the air took many shapes —some resembling the flying folds of a dress.

The old man saw it all and smiled.

He played and played with a smile in his eyes —and on his lips.

Night by Myself

So that thing is supposed to record my voice, eh? Why can't I just say everything I want straight to your face?

When we were newlyweds, you wanted to be with me all the time. You didn't want me to travel on my own. You refused to skyrocket your career because that meant being away from me. Now that seems like a long time ago. Since you took this new job, you travel a lot. Imagine how that makes me feel.

I love you, but I'm pissed at you. You're never here, and that doesn't seem to bother you. Every week you're out several nights.

Do I suspect you're cheating on me? Yes, I do. I've seen you talking to a guy outside our door. I've seen him so often I even have a nickname for him. I call him Stubble. Almost as tall as the door frame, shoulders just as wide. He combs his hair straight back, with lots of gel, and his beard is an eternal three-day stubble. I wonder how he does it. Does it ring a bell? What worries me most is that he looks at you with lust. I trust you, you wouldn't —not while I'm still here.

I keep thinking about the other night. I was asleep, enjoying the bed all to myself when the warmth in my feet awakened me. It was you, getting in bed.

"Did they cancel the trip?" I asked. I admit I didn't turn. I just wanted to go back to sleep.

"I really miss you, Tom," you said.

"I miss you too, babe."

"Sometimes, I feel like you're here when I speak to you, but then — you're not." You sighed.

"What's that supposed to mean?" I regretted it the moment I said it. I expected you would start bickering about how real men genuinely listen to women. I braced for the barrage that was coming, but nothing happened.

Then I felt you shaking softly on the bed beside me, "Honey?" I said, and I heard you whimper.

"Oh God, I wish you were really *here*, with *me*," you said between sobs.

"You know I love you, right? You're just tired," I said, turning to face you. You were holding a photo of our wedding and staring at it.

"I know you told me you would never even date again if anything happened to us, Tom. But I have to."

"Are you telling me you're seeing someone?" I yelled, but you took your time before responding.

"God. I can't," you said, "It's too soon."

"Are you telling me you want us to split?" I asked, but you didn't answer; you just kept sobbing, looking at the photo.

Do you remember? What was that about? And then tonight you come back here with this box and tell me that you want to know what I have to say. C'mon, what is this?

Is that the doorbell? What the hell is Stubble doing here? Wait a second, why is he holding you? Why are you kissing him? Hello? What is this, a prank? Why are you so surprised I threw that glass? What the hell do you expect?

Get out of my house, you moron. Get the hell out, you have no reason to be here. God, I never thought you would do this. What are you thinking? What about my feelings?

Don't take his hand. Please don't. Please don't. Oh God. I'm going to leave.

Why is the door locked? Am I stuck in here? Oh, God, no. I'm not watching. I'll wait in the living room. Just a moment. No, I can't let you sleep in our bedroom with him and do nothing about it. What kind of man would I be?

No, no, no, NO. Stop. Don't do it. Oh, God. I should've stayed in the living room. God. Get out of my bed. Leave my wife alone, you freak. You don't even feel my punches, do you? I'll give you something to try. Oh, I'm sorry, did I break your concentration? Shiver babe, shiver, you didn't expect me to be this mad, eh? What the hell did you expect? Oh yeah, you cover your breasts now, as if that makes you less of a slut. Tomorrow morning I want you out of this apartment. Tomorrow. No, wait, why should you wait until tomorrow, get out right now. Right now. Go, before I throw you out.

What the hell do you mean by "he doesn't know that he's dead"? Of course, I'm not dead, you idiot. I wouldn't be talking to you. No, no, keep that machine away from me. I don't want you to jolt me. Don't get so near. Don't. I must be dreaming. Are you a ghost? Why can't I touch you? Why do you get goosebumps when I try to touch you? Are both of you ghosts?

What's that light?

Am I the ghost?

[Male sobbing.]

Longest Electronic Voice Phenomenon (EVP) ever recorded by paranormal researchers in a house purported to be haunted.

Neighbors

Everything began with a knock on the door. It was a timid knock followed by other similar ones in a roll. It was my neighbor. He wasn't that old, fifty maybe, European, wrinkles like coarse bark, skin the color of anchovies. I mention it because when I opened the door on that day, he looked paler than usual.

"Hello, Mr. Constantinescu," I said.

My daughter grabbed my pants from behind and took a peek. She saw who it was, and continued playing with my son.

"What can I do for you?"

"Hello, my mother-in-law came to visit, so we're going to take her on a road trip. We'll be out for a few days. Would you be able to look after our house?"

He offered me a bunch of keys in a ring. A rabbit's foot was attached to the key-chain.

"Sure," I said, "but keep the rabbits' foot. I don't want to steal all your luck."

Mr. Constantinescu laughed and waved his hand, "Keep it, old beliefs, nothing but mumbo-jumbo."

"Here's the alarm code," he said and handed me a small note, "I'm going to leave it on. The alarm company should be able to turn it off if they need to, but—anyway, here it is."

As soon as I had taken the note, I saw something behind Mr. Constantinescu that looked like a pile of rags as high as my elbow. It's hard for me to describe it, but it looked like a round bale of hay with half a dome of rags on top of it.

As I stared at it, trying to figure out what it was, a head emerged from the dome of rags and directed its dull eyes toward me. The light-grey eyes were human, even if the white part was yellowish. What I had taken for a dome of rags was a hump. The person's skin was peculiar, too; in comparison, my neighbor's skin looked like a newborn's.

Mr. Constantinescu must've seen me staring behind him, because he turned around.

"Oh! There she is," he said, "my mother-in-law." He made it sound as if he was disappointed she was still there.

I greeted her by raising the palm of my hand as if I was about to high-five her. I didn't want to shake her hand, hell I didn't want to touch her. Call me squeamish, racist, whatever, but it wasn't like that. When I was little, my Dad made me shake hands with the old ladies at the retirement home. It felt like touching something that's not entirely alive anymore. It was like touching death. Maybe if I held too many old hands, I would catch —*death* – and die.

His mother-in-law talked rapidly in a language that sounded somewhat Latin but wasn't Spanish, nor Italian.

"Please forgive her," said my neighbor, "she's from Ardelan. She only speaks Romanian."

"Nice to meet you, Ma'am," I said, "enjoy your trip."

My daughter came from behind me to see who was talking. The old lady took an immediate interest in her, and a squalid white-as-bone arm reached out to touch her. My daughter squirmed behind me, trying to avoid her.

The woman said something in Romanian, and Mr. Constantinescu answered something brief while moving his hands up-and-down as if playing basketball defence. It seemed to me, he was trying to calm her.

"Pay no attention to my mother-in-law," my neighbor said, "but she wants to greet the child. I know children are not used to shaking hands with their elders anymore. Just ask her for appearance's sake, will you?"

I turned around to look for my daughter and found her hiding behind the door.

"Sweetie, would you mind saying hi to Mr. Constantinescu's mother-in-law?" I asked.

My daughter stood still. After what looked like a significant effort, she peeped from behind the door, and shook her head, while she looked at the old lady.

"Does that mean you don't mind?" I asked, but then the old lady reached for my daughter again, and my little one rushed into the house, screaming, "Moooom!" I wasn't going to force her. I wouldn't make my daughter do something that I wasn't willing to do myself.

Modern life being what it is, I forgot about having to look after my neighbor's house, until one evening my wife called from the stairs.

"Weren't the neighbors gone?"

"They were," I said.

"There's a light on."

I climbed the stairs to the landing, where my wife was looking out the window. The neighbors' curtains were closed, but through a gap, I could see the light inside.

"Maybe they just left it on."

"I'm going to take these to the laundry room," my wife said and walked away. I was returning to my chores when another light came on — this one, nearer to the window.

The first thought that came into my mind was that they had cut short their vacation and had forgotten to tell us about it. I didn't want to worry my neighbor unnecessarily, so I texted him. How's the vacation going?

After a few moments, I got my answer:

Great! We're really enjoying ourselves. Thanks for asking. Is everything ok?

What could I say? I wrote back, Sure. Keep enjoying it. Sleep Tight.

I called out loud for my wife to hear me, "Do you think they left the alarm on?"

I knew the answer before she said anything. They always left the alarm on. Always.

Then the lights went off.

The next night at about the same time, I was going up the stairs, when I saw a light illuminating my neighbor's living room. Maybe it was just my imagination, but the gap between the curtains seemed wider tonight. A few moments afterward, the second light turned on again. *They must have left the lights connected to a timer,* I thought. Then both lights went off at the same time.

But the living room wasn't thrown into complete darkness. I could see the flames from the fireplace playing shadow games on the walls. By that light, I thought I saw a mat of hair move through the gap in the curtains. It might have been someone squatting as to avoid detection, with only the hair showing. It might have been the mother-in-law, but then again, she was away on vacation.

I heard footsteps behind me. It was my wife. "They left the fireplace on. That's not safe. We have to turn it off," she said.

I knew she was right, but I didn't want to go in there. I'm not sure why. The memory of my dad making me shake hands with the old ladies flashed into my mind. I had a bad feeling. My wife saw me hesitating, "You don't have to go if you don't want to." Her words convinced me to go.

We checked on our kids before leaving. They were fast asleep. We took a flashlight and a baby monitor, which we still used. I typed 9-1-1 on the phone and placed my thumb over the SEND button. I nodded and said, "ready." I looked up from the phone and saw my wife shaking her head.

We opened the door, and the alarm started beeping. I disabled the alarm, raised the flashlight into the room, and saw the red dot on a motion sensor. They were active. If there were anything in here, the sensors would have picked it up.

We turned on the lights. Everything looked ok, except that the fireplace was still on. My wife turned it off while I unplugged the lamps that turned on every night. They weren't attached to a timer, and faulty wiring can start a fire.

I looked over my wife's shoulder. Through the gap in the curtains, I could see our house. A shadow was climbing up our staircase. "Look, our stairs," I said, turning her around.

"What?"

Then the monitor blared with the cry of my daughter.

We crossed our front yard as fast as we could. I ran up our stairs to her room.

She was sitting on her bed, grabbing her teddy bear. Tears streaked down her cheeks. "It was here, daddy. I saw her. She was here," she sobbed," I'm going to be a good girl now, daddy. Don't. Don't let her. Don't let her take me away."

I held her against my chest and hugged her. "You are a good girl, sweetie. No one is going to take you away." I heard my wife closing the door to our son's room.

"He's ok," she said from the door, and then faced my daughter, "Don't worry, sweetheart, nobody was here; it was only a nightmare."

I was sure I had seen something. It might have been just a shadow, but I stayed with my daughter all night. I fell asleep, hugging her.

The next evening, no lights were coming from the neighbor's house. Nothing seemed out of place, so my wife and I decided to have a movie night.

Half-way through the movie, we heard a rhythmical creaking coming from the stairs to the upper floor. It sounded as if someone was slowly, and silently, trying to reach the bedrooms. My wife and I looked at each other and then rushed up the stairs.

There she was. We caught the neighbor's mother-in-law, as she was touching my daughter's duvet.

"Ma'am, you've got the wrong house," my wife said, but she kept trying to reach my daughter.

I held her by the wrist. My hand went numb, and as I held on, the dark numbness rushed up my arm. My heart skipped a beat, then another one. The edges of my vision became blurry, and the room seemed smaller. My peripheral vision was shrinking. The darkness reached my shoulder and was released into my chest. I felt it constricting my heart, like black frayed leather strips becoming tighter and tighter.

My knee crashed onto the floor as I collapsed. I saw everything lopsided through a black tunnel. I tried sucking air to breathe and couldn't. My innards were paralyzed. A ringing in my ears blocked all sounds. I had to do something soon, or I would die. I called my wife but emitted no sound. I reached into my pocket for my phone and found the rabbit's foot. As soon as I touched it, the darkness fled. I've just had a heart attack, I thought.

"Your son-in-law will be here in no time Ma'am," my wife said, but when I looked for the old lady, she wasn't there.

"Where is she?" she asked. Her hands were facing up as if she had been holding something that had suddenly disappeared.

"Don't know," I gasped. "Did you see her leave?"

My wife and I locked eyes. She shook her head.

"Neither did I."

We called the neighbors, but no one answered. I stayed with my kids while my wife went to the neighbors' house. She didn't get past the doorbell. I don't blame her.

The next day, I heard the neighbor's garage being opened. I rushed out to meet them. They were dressed in black, and the mother-in-law wasn't with them.

"She passed away peacefully in her sleep," Mr. Constantinescu said.

"I'm really sorry for your loss," I said. "When did it happen?"

"Two nights ago. We would've returned yesterday, but the mortician didn't get there on time."

"I see," I said.

"Anything happened while we were out?"

I shook my head as I returned his keys.

I've kept the rabbit's foot.

Out of Whistler

I was late picking up my wife and our friends George and Stephanie. On top of that an ambulance and a fire truck were blocking the corner where I was supposed to pick them up.

I couldn't park there, and with all the traffic it was going to be tedious going around the block looking for them. Sometimes, Whistler is like that during the winter.

Then a voice startled me, "Hey, open the door."

It was George, and I was truly glad to see him. Now we could head back to Vancouver. With the touch of a button, the doors opened, and we were on our way.

"And what's that thing for?" George asked me as the four of us entered the Sea to Sky highway. He rode next to me, while our wives had taken the back seats of the van.

"Oh, that's just a camera," my wife said, pointing at the little lens on the windscreen. "Here you have to prove you did nothing wrong in case of an accident."

"But it doesn't record everything we're saying, does it?" Stephanie, asked.

"It sure does," I said.

George gave a low chuckle.

"Oh, I would never have it on. You never know what people can do with it," Stephanie said.

Daylight was fading. The lane stripes on the road were brighter than everything else around us, including the snow.

I heard the rumble of gossip from the back.

"Will there be traffic when we get to Vancouver?" George said.

"There won't be any traffic for us," I said, "we can use the HOV lane."

"With you being so late, the HOV hours might be over," my wife said and sank back into her one-on-one conversation with Stephanie.

The sun was already scraping the horizon as we drove between two snowy mountain peaks. Then we took a curve and one of the pine-studded slopes blocked the sun and it was almost as dark as night.

In the distance, we saw a traffic light.

George and I were silent as we approached the intersection. The green glow from its traffic light extended for a few meters around it, and just where the darkness was swallowing everything again, *we saw them.*

A man and a woman were hitchhiking. Their clothes seemed from another time. I thought they looked like run-away Amish, him wearing overalls and straw hat, her a black dress and bonnet. But there was something else. The woman stooped as if she carried a burden, and the rings around her eyes were so deep and black, they looked like the night around us was seeping through them. She exuded a sadness I have hardly ever seen before.

We were silent for a while, then George said, "That was creepy."

"It sure was. Why the hell would they be hitchhiking where it was so dark? If they'd been next to the light, maybe some good Samaritan would. . ."

"Hell, I would never have stopped. Not even for a million bucks. — They really looked creepy. If it had been Halloween. . . "

"It isn't."

"Yeah, you're right."

We left the conversation like that, but the feeling didn't abandon me. When we crossed the bridge into Vancouver, and the city lights surrounded us in every direction, George brought it up again. "They sure looked creepy, didn't they?"

"They sure did," I said.

"Dude — do you believe in ghosts?" George asked.

"We're grown up, c'mon. Of course I don't believe in ghosts. They were just two creepy looking sad runaways. That's all. We've got a lot of homeless around these parts."

"If you say so," George said. "I've always wondered if ghosts know they are dead. Maybe they just keep doing the things they did in life. I mean really, how would you know?"

In front of us, the real traffic started. Three of the four lanes were not moving. Only the HOV lane was free, so I took it.

"Anyway, I shouldn't worry about them," I said, "Hitchhiking is illegal. I'm sure the cops are going to catch them sooner or later."

I had just finished saying this when a police siren blared behind us. Through the rearview mirror, I saw a police car with its lights flashing. I pulled over so the patrol car would be able to pass. To my surprise it stopped right behind me.

"Good evening, Sir," I said when the officer stood next to my window and asked for my papers. "If you don't mind me asking, Sir—why did you stop me?"

"Beg your pardon?" he said, "You're on your own and in an HOV lane."

"What do you mean I'm alone," I said and chuckled, "what about them." I turned to face the passenger seat.

There was no one sitting there.

I turned on the interior lights; the women were gone too.

I got to the police station, handcuffed and sedated, and after insisting for hours that I had proof that I wasn't alone, the officer finally brought out the memory card from the van's dashcam and played the video.

The officer fast-forwarded the video to the part where I had seen the vagrants. There was no sound while the video sped forward.

"Here they come. Look to the right," I said.

The video slowed down. The traffic light came and went, and there was nothing to be seen.

"See. There was nothing there! There are no ghosts," the officer said.

I remembered what I had told George about not believing in ghosts.

Maybe I had mistaken the intersection for another one, but then we heard George's voice over the speakers, "that was creepy." And then my own, "It sure was. Why the hell would they be hitchhiking where it was so dark?"

The recording continued. Eventually the officer's voice came on the speakers, "Beg your pardon? —You're on your own and in an HOV lane."

I looked at him. I could tell he was as confused as I was.

Someone knocked on the door. The officer stopped the video and walked away. I kept staring at the screen, hoping to find a reflection on the windshield, something, anything that would help me explain what had happened.

Through the open door, I heard the clatter of the office, telephones ringing, and someone close by angrily hitting the buttons on a computer's keyboard.

"Would you mind repeating for me the names of the people that allegedly accompanied you in the vehicle?" He said when he came back.

"I wouldn't mind at all, Sir" I said and started repeating them for him, but he interrupted me.

"You said you were to pick them up, but the corner was blocked by a fire truck and an ambulance, right?"

I nodded.

"I know this is the worst day of your life. I wouldn't ask anything else from you if it was not completely necessary, but I need you to come to Whistler with me. I need you to ID their bodies."

Bonus Story

DEAD MAN'S BOOTS

"We are positively puzzled. After being a five-time national snowboard champion, you left the slopes," the reporter's blood-red lip dropped to reveal her perfect teeth. She frowned while she looked at me and shook her head a little. "You were the man. What happened?" She pushed the mike with the local TV's logo into my face.

"Why don't I go to the mountains anymore? You want to know why after such a successful career, I left it all without giving it a second thought?" I asked.

She nodded. She batted her full, thick, artificial eyelashes at me. I hated her guts, fake on top of fake.

 "I'll tell you," I said, "you're going to think I'm crazy, but maybe then *you people* will leave me alone."

She nodded.

"After I won the freestyle tournament, that year, I believed I could do anything. There wasn't a challenge I wasn't willing to take. I had plenty of money from all the sponsors that wanted me to represent their brands."

"Yes, you made more in a year than what most people would in their whole careers," the reporter said. "Don't you miss that?"

I closed my eyes, so that she wouldn't see them rolling up and pushed a finger to the bridge of my nose. "As I said: there wasn't a challenge, a dare, I wasn't willing to take. I felt indestructible."

"Dare…?," she asked.

"Yeah, like in High-School, I know. Really mature," I answered. I could see her judging me from behind those batting eyelashes. "Don't interrupt me, okay. It's already hard for me as it is."

"Sure. Sorry," she said, but it was evident she didn't regret it.

"We, my friends and I, usually went snowboarding for fun on the mountains in BC. There was a small resort we especially loved. Secluded, but at the same time close enough to Vancouver to come and go on the same day. They were always with me, we were a tight pack. At least I thought we were. I haven't seen them since…"

I felt a knot in my throat. So much for close friends. When you're at the top, everybody wants to hang with you. When you're not, everything changes.

The reporter nodded me to continue.

"We went there so often that we knew almost everyone in the alpine center.We were gearing up to go out, surrounded by the racks of rental gear."

"What's really the matter with those boots, man?" my friend Carl said, sticking up a finger that pointed vaguely at the top shelf of the equipment rack.

They were peculiar because they had a broad masking-tape on the back. A single word was written once for each boot. The word was DEAD.

"Ouuuuuh! Ze det man's booutz," Mike said, aiming for a Bela Lugosi accent.

"UUUUH!" We sang choir-like.

"Did anyone from the staff tell you anything about them?" Carl asked.

"Nah," I said, "I've already asked everyone. The boots have been here for years."

"I saw a lady cleaning them the other day," said Mike dropping his fake accent, "I was sure someone had to be cleaning them. Strange, though."

"What?"

"She never actually touched them. She passed the duster over them, but she didn't move them a single millimetre from where they were," Mike said, " as if she was afraid of them."

My friends and I, group-faked a shiver and settled down to get our gear on.

"Hey guys, wait. Eddy is here," Carl said, "let's see if he can come with us."

"Come on, man, we don't need him. We'll have more fun if we don't have to wait for him," I said.

The sound carried, and Eddy heard. "Well, maybe the rest of the world is not as fast as the champion, but we're here to have fun, aren't we guys. Besides, you've been lucky, wait until some of the real champs show up. Then we'll see if you're as good as you think you are."

If envy tinged people, Eddie would've been green.

"Whatever," I said.

"Or maybe when the real snow-gods come calling you won't even compete against them. You'll chicken out."

"Is that right?" I said, "name a challenge. I'll do it. I'll race you anywhere, anytime."

"I never said I was a good snowboarder," Eddie said, "I was thinking of something that proves once and for all what a chicken you are." He clucked and fluttered his elbows.

My friends, *my friends* laughed. They laughed!

I stood tall, looked him in the eye, and raised my arm. "Bring it on, "I said as I gestured with my fingers toward me.

"Do you see those boots," he paused for effect, "they belonged to a guy that was killed while going down the mountain. They are haunted. That's why no one will take them down from that rack."

We were in a tight semicircle around the rack with the boots. Everyone was looking at me.

"What does that have to do with me?" I said.

"How about going down the mountain with them?"

"Are you crazy? I'm pretty sure they're not even my number," I said.

"See," he said, "I told you he was yellow."

I shook my head and reached for one of the boots. Everyone gasped. I turned them around to see the size I was just trying to prove they weren't my size. To my surprise —they were.

Then Eddie took one of my boots, and chanted out loud, "Yours are nine and a half. Are the dead man's boots the same size as yours?"

We were so close that they could see the markings on the boot I was holding.

"I told you they would be," Mr. Envy said, "legend says they're always the size of the person that grabs them."

"Hmmm. Right," I said, trying to force a chuckle. I fought against the reflex to swallow, but I did anyway.

"Backing-off?" He said.

That was it for me. I looked around. No one from the staff was looking our way. They were too busy helping people into their skis and snowboards. I tore off the masking tape from the boots.

"I'll take them down the first run," I said, "and you'll take them for the second one. Unless you are a chicken yourself. You said the boots will take the size of the person holding them, so don't tell me the size will be an issue."

Eddie didn't say anything, he just nodded doubtfully.

I sat down to try them on. As I cleaned the inside of the boots, I noticed a name written in permanent marker: BILL STEADLER. I put them on, pumped them to fit nicely, and adjusted my board.

We took the first lift, and with anger and adrenaline pumping through my veins, I took the second one, and then the third one to the top of the mountain. Almost no one took the third lift. It was old and rickety, and most runs going down from there were the most dangerous.

When we all reached the top, trusting my skill, I said, "I'm going down the Devil's Fall," and pointed to the double-diamond black signpost to my right, "You sissies can go down that blue one, so you can see how real men do it."

My friends started clapping and mock-barking to cheer me on. Eddie looked sick.

I lowered the visor on my helmet, adjusted the chin-strap, and after checking everything was okay with my board and shoes, jumped right into the Devil's Fall.

The run started with an abrupt fall, which was a little wider than a board's length. I had to zig-zag my way down, avoiding rocky outcrops. It was almost jumping down with one side, then turning immediately to the other and then back again. I felt like a very quick pendulum moving regularly from one side to the other.

Then the pendulum became irregular, and I had to change my route midway to avoid the rocks right in the middle of the tight run. I was snowboarding like the gods.

I didn't feel quite the same without my shoes though, the curves weren't as tight as I would like them to be, and the board seemed to behave better if I jumped switching sides than if I tried to turn. As I was avoiding another rock in the run, my board slid, and I had to jump over a boulder to dodge it. The boots didn't transmit my movements as precisely as I would have liked. I had to jump over the next two stones. That meant that I was picking up speed instead of braking with each cut the board made on the snow.

That didn't worry me that much because the first leg of the run ended not so far below, and there was a small uphill section where I could easily break. I just needed to steer clear of the significant drop to my right called Skydiver's Paradise.

I kept jumping my way through the run, confident that I would be able to stop. I was on the right side of the slope, ready to take that last turn left that would get me away from the Skydiver's Paradise, when my foot moved back of its own accord, pushing me right instead of left. I struggled with all my might to turn the other way. Finally, when it was unavoidable, I thought I would let myself fall down so that my body's contact with the snow stopped my descent. I just needed a patch of snow without rocks. Then I realized this was a double-diamond black run; there weren't going to be many spots without stones. If I didn't slow down, I was going to be forced into the Skydiver's Paradise; without a way to make tight turns, that would be suicide. I made one last attempt to turn left by using all of my weight to change direction. My board was running on rocks now. Then a pebble broke loose, and with it, my board slid into the chasm on my right.

I was no longer snowboarding but sliding downhill, striving to avoid the sharpest rocks when I could see them. My back was flat against the mountain in the nearly vertical drop. Each time a stone hit me, I froze with the pain. My gloves were getting peeled by the jagged mountainside; I guessed all my clothes were. Due to my position, I couldn't see where I was going. I felt like I had left the run, but there was no way of telling. I pushed myself up, trying to regain control. From my point of view, everything in front of me looked as if seen from an airplane: miniature Douglas firs, pines, snow plows the size of ants. I was about to fall from a cliff.

I'm not going to make it, I thought.

Then I saw a lone pine tree, its roots like claws grabbing an outcrop on the mountain. I lunged for it, not minding about pain anymore. I grabbed one of the roots with one hand and pulled myself closer to the tree. As soon as I had caught the pine tree with my other hand, I felt a tug at my feet. Something was pulling at my board beyond gravity.

I looked down and saw an almost translucent form as if made from snow carried by the wind. It had the shape of a young man about my age. His feet used the same space as my feet, but he was standing up. Every time the shape pulled toward the cliff, I felt a tug on my feet. He kept pulling harder and harder, and I was afraid I was going to lose my grip on the tree. But then he pulled extremely hard, and somehow my board came off. I gathered all my strength and managed to pull myself up. I hugged the tree, mounting it like a horse. I kept feeling the tugs on my feet, but with the tree between my legs, they were easier to resist. I hoped the tree would hold. With one hand, I unbuckled one boot and saw it tumble down for a short distance, only to lose sight of it as it plummeted into oblivion. I took the other one off, and then the tugging stopped.

In my socks, I climbed up to where the Skydiver's Paradise started. There was a small plaque on the rightmost side of the slope. It said:

IN LOVING MEMORY

OF

BILL STEADLER

1982-2003

Acknowledgements

I want to thank my editor and friend Erik D'Souza, who taught me again how to write.

To my friends from the Port Moody Writer's Group especially Eileen Kernaghan for giving me the support I needed to thrive.

To Rene Romero & Rodrigo Montiel for believing in me, and seeing potential where I saw none.

To my Sarmiento family who's always behind me.

To my band of brothers, The Society. For years you were my first and only audience, with you I became the storyteller I am today.

To all my friends, for being there for me.

Biography

Lozano Gilabert studied and worked as a psychotherapist for nearly twelve years before becoming a writer. Lozano Gilabert spent many Friday evenings at one of Mexico's main psychiatric hospitals interviewing patients. Some say his stories are based on what was learned through those interviews.

Lozano Gilabert's family haunt the Lower Mainland in British Columbia, Canada, along with a hellhound named BonBon.

Lozano Gilabert is the author of more than fifty stories and screenplays.

More spooky stories will be coming soon. *Creatures from the Dark* will be available early 2021

Learn more at clozanogilabert.com